Whispers of Deception Bloodlines Unveiled

Richard Porter

Published by Richard Porter, 2023.

WHISPERS OF DECEPTION BLOODLINES UNVEILED

First edition. May 15, 2023.

Copyright © 2023 Richard Porter.

ISBN: 979-8223934981

Written by Richard Porter.

Table of Contents

Chapter 1:"Untangling the Enigma: Unveiling the Veiled Secrets!"

My heart goes out to you, Ethan, as I sit here, pen in hand, pouring my emotions onto the blank canvas of this letter. Even though I do not know you, the weight of our shared pain and uncertainty connects us in a way that words alone cannot express.

In the quiet solitude of my small room, surrounded by the echoes of a town oblivious to the turmoil within my soul, I find solace in the ink-stained pages that will bridge the vast chasm between us. As the pen glides across the paper, it carries with it the weight of my shattered dreams and the flickering hope that lingers in the depths of my wounded heart.

With each stroke of my pen, the truth unravels before me, thread by agonizing thread. Our innocent correspondence, once a flicker of curiosity and hope, has transformed into a vessel for the revelation of a devastating secret. A secret that taints the very foundation upon which our lives were built—a deception that cuts deep into the core of our being.

Lily's hands trembled as she recalled the moment when the fragile facade began to crumble, revealing the painful truth that lay hidden beneath the surface. The letters exchanged between her and Ethan, innocent at first, had unveiled a tangled web of betrayal and familial ties. With each new revelation, their lives spiraled further into a darkness they could never have imagined.

Ethan's words, penned with an equal measure of desperation and disbelief, echoed through Lily's mind. They had discovered that their spouses were not simply unfaithful, but rather, long-lost siblings entangled in a clandestine affair. The weight of this realization pressed down upon them, threatening to suffocate the remnants of their shattered hearts.

How could this be? The question reverberated within Lily's mind, shattering the fragments of her once idyllic existence. The love that had bound them together now seemed to mock them, transformed into a cruel and bitter twist of fate. The life they had built with their spouses—the dreams, the memories, the shared laughter—now lay tainted, like shards of a broken mirror reflecting their shattered reflection.

In the wake of this revelation, Lily and Ethan could no longer cling to the innocence they had once possessed. Their letters became a refuge—a sanctuary where they could untangle the web of deceit, one word at a time. Through their shared pain, they forged an unbreakable bond, providing solace and strength to one another as they faced the harsh reality that awaited them.

As each letter exchanged hands, the weight of their emotions grew heavier, like stones tied to their souls. They embarked on a treacherous journey, uncovering buried secrets and exposing the darkness that lay hidden within their family's history. With each revelation, they were torn between their love for their spouses and the horrifying truth that threatened to tear their lives apart.

Lily and Ethan's correspondence became a lifeline, a fragile thread connecting their broken hearts. Through tear-stained words and heartfelt confessions, they found solace in their shared sorrow. Their letters became a testament to their resilience, a testament to the indomitable spirit that refused to succumb to the shadows that loomed over them.

In the face of such heart-wrenching betrayal, Lily and Ethan would discover that sometimes, the greatest strength lies in embracing the truth, no matter how painful. With their lives entwined in this unforeseen twist of fate, they would uncover the depths of their own courage, resilience, and the capacity to heal wounds that ran soul-deep.

Little did they know, as they poured their hearts into their letters, that their words held the power to change not only their own lives but the lives of those they loved. Their words became a catalyst, a force that would shake the very foundations of their intertwined families and propel them toward a truth that demanded to be heard.

As the correspondence deepened, Lily and Ethan could no longer ignore the gnawing questions that lingered in their hearts. They began to unravel the intricate tapestry of their shared lineage, unearthing secrets that had been meticulously hidden away, like ghosts lurking in the shadows of their family history.

Through tear-stained pages, they pieced together the fragments of a haunting tale—a tale of long-lost siblings torn apart by a tragedy they had never known, a tragedy that had cast its dark shadow over their lives without their knowledge. The very blood that coursed through their veins, the blood that had once united them in love, now seemed tainted, stained with the sins of their ancestors.

With each revelation, their anguish grew, fueling an insatiable hunger for the truth. Their search for answers took them to the depths of the past, where buried memories and half-forgotten whispers revealed a lineage plagued by deception and pain. They discovered the bitter legacy that had been passed down, from generation to generation, an inheritance of secrets that had scarred their souls.

The weight of the truth bore down upon them, threatening to shatter their fragile hearts. Yet, in the midst of the darkness, they found solace in their shared journey. They became each other's pillars of strength, their words weaving a tapestry of empathy, understanding, and unwavering support.

Through the depths of their pain, Lily and Ethan discovered an unexpected bond—a bond that transcended their initial connection, born out of desperation and uncertainty. It was a bond forged through vulnerability, as they bared their souls to one another, laying bare their deepest fears and insecurities.

In the midst of their turmoil, they found fleeting moments of solace, where laughter mingled with tears, and hope intertwined with despair. They clung to these moments, cherishing the fragile light that flickered amidst the encroaching darkness. Their hearts, scarred but not broken, sought solace in the warmth of their shared connection.

As their journey neared its tumultuous climax, Lily and Ethan faced a crossroads—a choice that would shape the course of their lives forever. Would they succumb to the weight of the truth, allowing it to consume them in bitterness and resentment? Or would they rise above the shadows, armed with the power of forgiveness and a determination to forge a new path?

In the face of overwhelming odds, they chose love. Love not only for each other, but for the family they had unknowingly inherited—a family steeped in pain, yet capable of redemption. With their hearts heavy but resolute, they set out on a mission to confront their spouses, to confront the ghosts of their shared past, and to reclaim their own identities amidst the tangled web of deceit.

Their love became a beacon, guiding them through the stormy sea of emotions. It was a love that refused to be extinguished, even in the face of betrayal and shattered trust. It fueled their determination to uncover the truth, to heal the wounds that ran deep, and to build a future upon the fragile foundations of forgiveness and understanding.

As Lily and Ethan sealed their letters with tears and hope, they embarked on a journey that would forever change their lives. In the uncharted territory of their intertwined destinies, they found the strength to confront the darkness, to break the cycle of pain, and to embrace a newfound sense of purpose—a purpose that emerged from the depths of their shared anguish, blossoming into a story of resilience, redemption, and the enduring power of love.

Chapter 2: Echoes of Truth

The revelation struck Lily and Ethan like a tidal wave, shaking the very foundations of their existence. As they delved deeper into the mystery that had ensnared them, the fragile threads of their lives began to unravel before their tear-filled eyes.

In a dimly lit room, surrounded by old photographs and forgotten memories, Lily and Ethan unearthed the truth they had longed to know, yet feared to face. Their parents, the very pillars of their existence, had conspired in a clandestine affair, an affair that birthed their lives and forever linked their fates. Separated at birth, they were pawns in a dark game of secrets and deception.

The weight of the truth bore down on their hearts, leaving them breathless, their souls shredded by the betrayal of those they loved most. How could their parents, the very guardians who were meant to protect and guide them, orchestrate such a cruel charade? Their minds reeled, struggling to comprehend the magnitude of the web that had ensnared their lives.

Tears cascaded down Lily's cheeks as she traced her fingers over the faded photograph of her parents, her once idealized image of them crumbling beneath the weight of this revelation. The home she had known, the love she had cherished, all now tainted by the shadows of their hidden past. She clutched her chest, aching with the pain of shattered innocence and misplaced trust.

Ethan, his voice barely above a whisper, gazed at the face of his mother in an old family portrait. The woman who had nurtured and protected him, who had wiped away his tears and cheered him on, now seemed like a stranger. His heart ached with a mixture of fury and heartbreak, unable to reconcile the love he had felt with the deceit that now lay exposed.

Their minds raced with questions, a storm of emotions crashing against their fragile resolve. Should they confront their cheating spouses, laying bare the truth and tearing their families apart? Or should they guard the fragile stability they had fought so hard to maintain, protecting the innocence of their children at the cost of their own shattered hearts?

Lily and Ethan found solace in each other's embrace, their pain mingling as they clung to the only constants left in their lives. Their love, once hidden beneath the surface of friendship, now bloomed with an intensity they had never known. Together, they faced the storm, their hearts intertwined in a desperate dance of vulnerability and strength.

But amidst the chaos, a seed of resilience sprouted within them. A flicker of determination illuminated their tear-streaked faces as they vowed to rise above the brokenness that threatened to consume them. Their love for their children burned like a beacon, guiding them forward into an uncertain future.

As they stood on the precipice of truth, Lily and Ethan knew they had to make a choice. A choice that would redefine their lives, shatter the illusions they had clung to, and unravel the lies that had held them captive. But deep within the darkness, they found the flicker of hope, the belief that sometimes, the most painful truths lead to the most profound healing.

With trembling hands and resolute hearts, they steeled themselves for the battle ahead. The time for secrets was over, and the time for redemption had come. They would confront their cheating spouses, not for vengeance, but for the chance to rebuild their lives on the foundation of truth. In the face of adversity, they would forge a new path, one marked by forgiveness, resilience, and the unwavering strength of their love.

Together, they stepped into the unknown, their hearts heavy with the burdens of their past, yet brimming with the hope of a future yet to be written.

The air hung heavy with anticipation as Lily and Ethan prepared to confront their cheating spouses. The walls of their home, once a sanctuary of love and laughter, now seemed to close in on them, suffocating them with the weight of their shattered illusions. Each step felt like a struggle, as if the very ground beneath their feet threatened to give way.

Gathering their resolve, Lily and Ethan took a deep breath and entered the room where their spouses awaited them. The atmosphere crackled with tension, an electric current pulsating through the air. Their eyes met the eyes of their betrayers, and for a moment, time stood still.

Silence lingered, heavy and pregnant with unspoken words. Lily's voice trembled as she found the strength to break the deafening stillness. "We know the truth," she whispered, her voice barely audible. "We know about the affair. About the lies."

Her spouse, the person she had once shared her dreams and secrets with, avoided her gaze, unable to meet the piercing weight of her accusation. The truth had been unveiled, and the charade they had orchestrated had crumbled beneath the weight of their deceit.

Ethan's voice, a mixture of pain and determination, cut through the silence. "How could you?" he demanded, his voice quivering with a mixture of anger and sadness. "How could you betray us, your own flesh and blood? We were meant to be a family."

Their spouses shifted uncomfortably, their guilt-laden eyes unable to meet the devastation they had caused. The room seemed to close in on them, walls closing in like a prison, trapping them in the suffocating grip of their own actions.

But amidst the anguish and heartbreak, a glimmer of something unexpected emerged. Lily and Ethan, despite the pain that coursed through their veins, held onto a flicker of empathy. They saw their spouses as not just betrayers but as flawed individuals who had been swept up in their own web of lies.

Lily's voice softened, a delicate vulnerability shining through her tears. "We loved you," she murmured, her words filled with a longing for understanding. "We loved you despite your flaws, despite the mistakes we all make. But this... this was too much."

Ethan's eyes, filled with a mixture of sorrow and defiance, met his spouse's gaze. "We deserve better," he stated, his voice firm with resolve. "Our children deserve better. We won't let this define us or destroy our families."

In that moment, a seismic shift occurred within the room. It was not a moment of reconciliation or forgiveness, but a moment of liberation.

Lily and Ethan had made their choice—to protect the fragile stability of their families, to shield their children from the chaos that had unfolded.

As they turned their backs on their cheating spouses, tears mingled with the residue of shattered trust, leaving trails of pain and resilience. They walked away, their steps heavy but resolute, leaving behind the wreckage of broken vows and shattered dreams.

In the days and weeks that followed, Lily and Ethan faced the daunting task of rebuilding their lives, of reshaping the foundations on which their families stood. They immersed themselves in the love and support of friends and family, seeking solace in the warmth of those who stood by them unconditionally.

The journey ahead was arduous, and the wounds left by the revelation would take time to heal. But in their hearts, Lily and Ethan carried the seed of hope, the unwavering belief that amidst the wreckage, something beautiful could be born.

They learned to redefine the meaning of family, to embrace the connections that extended beyond blood and genetics. Lily and Ethan found solace and strength in each other

Lily and Ethan's bond grew stronger with each passing day, weaving a tapestry of love and understanding that transcended the pain of their shared past. Together, they navigated the tumultuous waters of healing, their hearts mending like fragile glass, but never losing sight of the beauty that could emerge from the shards.

As they delved into their shared history, they discovered the depth of their connection extended far beyond the revelations of their parents' betrayal. Their souls, entwined from the moment they first met, had always yearned for one another, silently seeking solace in the arms of their chosen family.

In the quiet moments of the night, they would lie intertwined, fingers tracing delicate patterns across each other's skin. Their whispered conversations filled the darkness, baring their deepest fears and dreams.

In each other's presence, they found sanctuary, a safe haven where vulnerability could bloom.

Through their journey of healing, Lily and Ethan discovered the power of forgiveness. It was not a simple act, nor did it come easily. It was a complex dance, a delicate interplay of anger, sadness, and the willingness to let go of the pain that bound them. They understood that forgiveness was not a justification for the past, but a way to set themselves free from its chains.

Their children, too young to understand the intricacies of their parents' struggle, became their guiding lights. Lily and Ethan vowed to shield them from the darkness that had once consumed their lives. They created a haven of love, where laughter and joy danced hand in hand with resilience and growth.

In the wake of the storm, Lily found solace in the arts. She poured her emotions onto the canvas, each brushstroke a testament to her journey of self-discovery. The colors she used were not always vibrant; they reflected the depth of her experience, the hues of anguish and hope merging into a masterpiece of healing.

Ethan, on the other hand, turned to the written word. Through his heartfelt prose, he found catharsis. His words danced across the pages, transforming pain into poetry and bitterness into wisdom. He shared his stories with others, offering a beacon of inspiration to those navigating their own tumultuous seas.

As time passed, Lily and Ethan realized that their story was not just about their pain and redemption; it was a testament to the resilience of the human spirit. Their journey touched the lives of others, creating ripples of hope that spread far beyond their own circle.

They became advocates for healing, using their own experiences to empower and uplift others who found themselves entangled in the web of deceit and betrayal. Through support groups and community outreach, they offered a lifeline to those who felt lost in the darkness, reminding them that they were not alone.

Though the scars of their past would always be a part of them, Lily and Ethan chose to embrace the beauty that emerged from their brokenness. They wove a new narrative, one built on the foundations of truth, forgiveness, and an unwavering commitment to love.

Their shared journey was a testament to the resilience of the human heart, a reminder that even in the face of unimaginable pain, there is always a glimmer of hope. And as they stood hand in hand, facing the horizon of their future, Lily and Ethan knew that their love, forged in the crucible of adversity, was unbreakable.

Chapter 3: Bond of Shared Pain

As the days turned into weeks and the weeks into months, Lily and Ethan's correspondence blossomed into something far more profound than either of them had anticipated. Their letters became a lifeline, a refuge in the storm of their troubled lives. They poured their hearts onto the pages, weaving a tapestry of emotions that bound them together with an unbreakable thread.

Lily, with her delicate penmanship, painted a vivid portrait of her shattered past. She revealed the pain of growing up in a home devoid of love, where her parents' indifference left her feeling like an abandoned ship lost at sea. With every stroke of her pen, she bared her soul, releasing years of pent-up anger, sorrow, and longing. And in those intimate moments shared through ink-stained letters, she found solace in Ethan's understanding gaze.

Ethan, scarred by his own history, offered Lily his compassionate heart. He described the constant ache he carried, born from a childhood spent in the shadow of his father's betrayal. The wounds were still fresh, a testament to the lasting impact of shattered trust. But as his words flowed onto the paper, a flicker of hope ignited within him. Through Lily's unwavering support, he dared to believe in the healing power of connection.

Their letters became a sanctuary, a realm where they could be their true selves without fear of judgment. They confided their deepest fears and wildest dreams, their hopes and desires, their darkest secrets. Their souls danced upon the parchment, revealing the intricacies of their wounded hearts.

In one particularly poignant letter, Lily unveiled a long-held secret that had plagued her for years. She confessed the weight of guilt she carried for her mother's untimely death. Tears stained the paper as she recounted the tragic accident that stole her mother away, the burden of responsibility etched in every word. She had blamed herself, believing that her presence had somehow cursed her mother's fate.

Ethan's heart shattered as he read her painful revelation. In that moment, he understood the depths of Lily's anguish, her relentless self-condemnation. With a trembling hand, he penned a response that echoed with empathy and compassion. He shared his own guilt, the weight of regret for the choices he couldn't undo. Together, they wove a tapestry of shared sorrow, their broken pieces fitting together like jagged shards of glass.

Their bond deepened, transcending the realm of friendship. It became a lifeline, an anchor in the midst of their storm- tossed lives. Through their shared pain, they discovered strength within themselves they never knew existed. They found courage to confront the demons that haunted them, to seek justice and redemption for the sins of their parents.

Their quest for truth became their shared purpose, a testament to the unyielding power of their connection. With every letter exchanged, their determination grew, fueled by the unwavering support they found in each other. Together, they became warriors, fighting against the shadows that threatened to consume them.

In their hearts, Lily and Ethan knew that their bond was forged in the fires of adversity. It was a love born from the depths of their shared pain, an unbreakable tether that defied the odds. And as they embarked on this treacherous journey, their intertwined hearts beat in unison, carrying them forward, united in their pursuit of justice and redemption.

As Lily and Ethan delved deeper into their quest, the emotional connection between them continued to flourish, defying the physical distance that separated them. Their hearts were intertwined, beating as one, even though their bodies remained miles apart.

With each passing day, their determination to uncover the truth burned brighter. Lily's letters overflowed with passion, her words infused with an unyielding desire to bring to light the secrets that had shrouded their lives. She detailed her tireless efforts to comb through old records, to follow any lead, no matter how faint, that could lead them closer to the truth.

Ethan, too, immersed himself in the search, driven by a newfound purpose that ignited his spirit. He tirelessly sifted through documents, tirelessly pursued connections, determined to unearth the buried secrets that held their families captive. And in those moments when exhaustion threatened to consume him, he found strength in Lily's words, her unwavering belief in their shared mission.

Their emotional bond became a lifeline amidst the darkness they encountered. In moments of doubt, they turned to each other, seeking reassurance and encouragement. Lily's letters dripped with love and tenderness, reminding Ethan of the light that burned within them, guiding their path. His replies echoed with devotion, reassuring her that they were in this together, that no obstacle would deter their pursuit.

But as they ventured deeper into the labyrinth of their parents' deception, their emotional bond was tested. They uncovered painful truths that threatened to shatter their fragile hearts. Secrets so devastating that the weight of them threatened to extinguish their flame of hope.

One night, Lily's hand trembled as she poured her anguish onto the paper. She confessed a discovery that tore at the very fabric of her being. It was a revelation that implicated her own father in a web of lies and deceit, a betrayal that cut deeper than any wound she had known before. Her heart bled onto the page, stained with the agony of shattered trust.

Ethan's heart constricted as he read Lily's words, feeling her pain reverberate through his own veins. He cradled the letter in his hands, his soul tormented by the realization that the darkness they sought to conquer lurked within their own families. With a heavy heart, he penned a reply, his words a balm for their wounded spirits. He promised to stand by her side, to face their shared demons head-on, no matter the cost.

And so, armed with their intertwined hearts and a determination that burned brighter than ever, Lily and Ethan pressed forward. Their journey became a pilgrimage of healing and transformation, a testament to the power of love and resilience. They confronted their parents' sins with a ferocity born from their shared pain, refusing to let the weight of their legacy define them.

In the depths of their souls, they knew that their emotional bond had become their lifeline, their guiding star in a sea of darkness. Through every triumph and setback, they leaned on each other, finding solace in their shared vulnerability. They cried together, they laughed together, and they fought together, united by a love that had been forged in the crucible of their broken pasts.

And as they stood on the precipice of the truth they sought, their hearts intertwined more tightly than ever before. They were no longer just confidants; they were kindred spirits, intertwined souls who had found salvation in each other's embrace. In their letters, they discovered the true power of connection, the transformative force that could mend even the deepest wounds.

Together, Lily and Ethan embraced the unknown, fueled by the indomitable strength of their love. And as they took their first steps into the realm of truth, their intertwined hearts beat as one.

The road to truth was treacherous, with unforeseen twists and painful revelations testing Lily and Ethan's resilience at every turn. The weight of their shared burden grew heavier, threatening to crush their spirits. But in those moments of despair, they found solace in each other's arms, their emotional bond serving as an anchor in the storm.

As they delved deeper into the labyrinth of secrets, Lily's nights became restless, haunted by nightmares of her past. The weight of her mother's death and her father's betrayal bore down on her, threatening to suffocate her spirit. In the midst of her anguish, she turned to the only source of solace she knew: Ethan's letters. They became her lighthouse, guiding her through the tempestuous sea of emotions.

Ethan, too, faced his own inner demons. Doubt gnawed at his resolve, whispering that their quest for justice was futile. The darkness of his father's deeds cast a long shadow over his heart, and he questioned whether redemption was truly attainable. But then he would receive a letter from Lily, brimming with unwavering faith and determination, reminding him of the fire that burned within them. Her words rekindled his spirit, igniting a renewed sense of purpose.

Their emotional bond became a refuge, a sanctuary where they could lay bare their fears and vulnerabilities. They shared their deepest scars, their darkest moments, and in doing so, they discovered that they were not alone in their pain. Their connection transcended the boundaries of friendship, evolving into a love that knew no bounds.

One stormy night, as Lily sat huddled by candlelight, the weight of her mother's death threatened to consume her. Tears streamed down her face, mingling with the ink on the page as she poured her heart out to Ethan. In that moment of vulnerability, she confessed her fear of never finding closure, of forever being trapped in the web of their parents' deception.

Ethan's heart shattered as he read her words, feeling her anguish echoing within his own soul. With trembling hands, he penned a response, his emotions flowing freely onto the paper. He vowed to be her anchor, her source of strength, as they navigated the storm together. His words carried the weight of his love, promising her that they would find the truth, no matter the cost.

In their shared pain, Lily and Ethan discovered a reservoir of untapped strength. They found the courage to confront their own demons, to face the shadows that had haunted their lives. With every step forward, their emotional bond deepened,

intertwining their hearts with an unbreakable thread.

The journey tested their resilience in ways they never imagined. They faced resistance, encountered those who sought to keep their secrets buried. But Lily and Ethan refused to be deterred. The fire within them burned brightly, fueled by their unyielding love and unwavering determination. Hand in hand, they ventured into the darkest recesses of their families' pasts, unearthing truths that threatened to tear them apart.

Yet, even as the revelations threatened to unravel them, Lily and Ethan clung to each other, their emotional bond a lifeline amidst the chaos. They found strength in the quiet moments of reassurance, in the understanding that they were not alone in their pain. Their love grew stronger with each obstacle overcome, each secret unraveled.

Together, they stood on the precipice of the truth they had so fervently sought. Their intertwined hearts beat in perfect harmony, their souls forever entwined. And as they finally laid bare the extent of their parents' deception, their emotional bond served as a guiding light, illuminating the path to justice and redemption.

In the end, it was their unbreakable emotional bond that propelled Lily and Ethan forward, through the final threshold of their journey. The truth stood before them, raw and unfiltered, a revelation that threatened to shatter their fragile hearts once more.

As they faced the culmination of their efforts, a mix of fear and anticipation gripped their souls. Their hands trembled as they prepared themselves to confront the depths of their parents' deception. But they found solace in knowing that they were not alone. Together, they would face the truth, no matter how painful.

Lily and Ethan stood side by side, their intertwined hearts beating in sync, as they unearthed the final pieces of the puzzle. The truth unfolded before them like a cruel tapestry, revealing the extent of their parents' lies and manipulations. The weight of it threatened to overwhelm them, but they clung to each other, drawing strength from their shared resolve.

In that moment of reckoning, Lily and Ethan realized that their quest for justice and redemption had not only been about their parents' sins but also about their own healing. The emotional bond they had nurtured had become a catalyst for their own growth and transformation. They had confronted their deepest fears, peeled back the layers of their own wounds, and found the courage to forgive and let go.

With tear-streaked faces and hearts brimming with a mixture of grief and liberation, they embraced the truth that had been denied to them for so long. The burden of their parents' sins was no longer theirs to carry alone. They had unearthed the buried secrets, shed light on the darkness, and paved the way for a future untainted by deceit.

As they stood on the precipice of a new chapter in their lives, Lily and Ethan's emotional bond remained unbreakable. Their hearts, scarred but resilient, beat with a renewed sense of purpose. They had forged a connection that transcended the confines of their shared past, a love that had weathered the storms of their journey.

In the aftermath of their revelation, Lily and Ethan chose different paths. Their lives diverged, leading them down separate roads of healing and growth. But their emotional bond endured, an invisible thread that connected them across distance and time.

In the years that followed, they continued to exchange letters, their words filled with love, gratitude, and the shared understanding of what they had overcome. They celebrated each other's triumphs and offered solace in moments of pain. Through their connection, they found solace and strength, forever grateful for the transformative power of their intertwined hearts.

And as they closed the chapter on their tumultuous past, they stepped into a future shaped by the healing power of love. Lily and Ethan emerged from the shadows of their parents' deception, their hearts forever entwined, a testament to the resilience of the human spirit and the redemptive nature of connection.

Chapter 4: Emotional Quest Begins

The world had shattered around them. Lily and Ethan thought they had unraveled the truth when they discovered their spouses' affair, but little did they know that the pain they had endured was just the beginning. As they delved deeper into the darkness, uncovering more evidence, their hearts sank further, and an indescribable heaviness settled upon them.

The room felt suffocating, its walls closing in on Lily and Ethan, as if mirroring their torment. The once familiar surroundings now seemed foreign, tainted by the secrets they had uncovered. Their hands trembled, holding the incriminating photographs and documents that revealed the clandestine organization orchestrating their lives.

In a desperate quest for answers, they had stumbled upon the truth that had eluded them for far too long. This clandestine organization, hidden in the shadows, had manipulated their destinies with calculated precision. Their marriages, their hopes, their dreams—all mere pawns in a wicked game of deceit.

The weight of the realization pressed heavily upon their hearts. It was not just their spouses who had betrayed them; it was an entire network of puppeteers pulling the strings. Anguish and disbelief mingled within them, like a storm brewing beneath their skin. How could this be? How could they have been so blind?

Tears streamed down Lily's face as she clutched the evidence to her chest. Her once bright eyes, now clouded with pain, searched Ethan's gaze for solace. They were two shattered souls, connected by the agony of betrayal and the determination to fight back against the forces that sought to control their lives.

Ethan's voice trembled with a mix of sorrow and resolve. "Lily, we can't let them win. We can't let them destroy everything we hold dear. Our love, our trust, it's all that's left. We have to expose this organization, for the sake of our sanity and for the countless others who might be trapped in their web."

A silent understanding passed between them, a shared commitment to bring down the invisible oppressors who had shattered their lives. Time seemed to blur, its significance heightened by the urgency of their mission. They were no longer two individuals wounded by betrayal; they were warriors bound by a common cause.

Days turned into nights as they meticulously pieced together the puzzle, connecting dots and unraveling the secrets that held the organization together. Each revelation struck them like a blow to the chest, but they refused to yield to despair. With every step forward, their determination grew, fueled by the fire of their broken hearts.

Their emotions were a maelstrom—fury, sorrow, and unyielding love swirling within them. Their journey had transformed from a pursuit of truth into a battle for their very souls. The weight of their discoveries threatened to break them, but it also ignited a fierce determination to break free from the clutches of those who sought to control their destinies.

Through the long nights and endless days, Lily and Ethan forged an unbreakable bond. They found strength in each other, drawing courage from the tender moments they shared amidst the chaos. It was a bittersweet solace, knowing that their love had endured the ultimate test, but had also been scarred by the lies they had uncovered.

And so, with their hearts heavy yet alight with resolve, Lily and Ethan prepared to face the world they once thought they knew. The organization's secrets were now theirs to expose, their love a shield against the darkness that threatened to consume them. Together, they would fight to reclaim their lives and to shatter the illusion that had ensnared them.

Their journey had just begun, and the road ahead was treacherous, but in their shared pain, they found a flicker of hope— a flame that refused to be extinguished. Their emotions ran deep, intertwining their souls as they braced themselves for the battle that lay ahead.

As they stepped out into the world, their footsteps carried the weight of countless shattered dreams and broken promises. With unwavering determination, they sought allies in the most unlikely of places, individuals who had also been ensnared by the organization's devious schemes. Together, they formed a fragile network of truth-seekers, united by the shared desire to expose the darkness that lurked in the shadows.

Every piece of evidence they gathered was a painful reminder of the lives torn asunder, the families ripped apart. The clandestine organization had spread its venomous tendrils far and wide, leaving destruction in its wake. Lily and Ethan's hearts bled for every soul entangled in the web of manipulation.

The more they unraveled, the clearer it became that their own pain was just a fraction of the suffering inflicted by the organization. Innocent lives had been shattered, destinies diverted, and love trampled upon. The weight of their mission grew heavier, but so did their resolve.

They reached out to victims who were too afraid to speak, offering a lifeline of support and understanding. They listened to stories of shattered dreams and stolen identities, tears mingling with the ink on their notepads. It was through these shared experiences that they found the strength to carry on, to fight for justice, and to reclaim their own identities that had been marred by deception.

The journey was not without its challenges. The organization, sensing the threat posed by their relentless pursuit of truth, deployed its formidable arsenal of manipulation and intimidation. Lily and Ethan faced threats to their safety, their

reputations tarnished by insidious rumors, and their every move tracked by unseen eyes.

But with each obstacle they overcame, their spirit grew stronger. Their love became a beacon of hope, guiding them through the darkest of nights. They refused to be silenced, refused to let fear dictate their actions. They had glimpsed the true face of evil, and they would not rest until it was unmasked for the world to see.

And so, armed with a tapestry of evidence and the unwavering support of those who had suffered alongside them, Lily and Ethan prepared to expose the organization's secrets. The truth would be their weapon, wielded with courage and resilience, cutting through the lies that had ensnared so many.

Their hearts raced with anticipation as they stood before the world, their voices trembling yet filled with unwavering conviction. The moment had come to unveil the hidden web of manipulation, to bring the perpetrators to justice, and to give voice to the voiceless. They were not just fighting for their own redemption, but for the countless lives shattered by the organization's malevolence.

As the truth spilled forth, like a torrential downpour washing away the lies, Lily and Ethan stood side by side, their hands tightly intertwined. They had emerged from the depths of betrayal, their souls scarred yet resilient. In that moment, they knew that their journey was not just about exposing an organization—it was about healing their own hearts and helping others find solace in the truth.

Their story would become a testament to the indomitable power of love, the unyielding strength of the human spirit, and the triumph over adversity. And as they gazed into each other's eyes, their hearts brimming with gratitude for the courage they had found within themselves, they knew that they had already won the most significant battle—the battle to reclaim their own lives and to forge a future built on the foundation of truth, love, and unwavering resilience.

Chapter 5: Embers of Resilience

Lily's heart pounded in her chest as she and Ethan ventured deeper into the treacherous maze of secrets and deceit. Their journey had transformed into a perilous odyssey, where danger lurked behind every turn, threatening to consume them whole. The weight of their mission settled heavily upon their shoulders, and the gravity of their task sent shivers down their spines.

As they pressed on, the landscape seemed to mirror the turmoil within their souls. The once vibrant meadows they traversed had given way to desolate wastelands, their beauty ravaged by the malevolence that gripped their world. Shadows danced eerily in the fading sunlight, whispering tales of treachery and deception that sent chills up their spines.

Yet, amidst the encroaching darkness, unexpected allies emerged from the depths of despair. A weary old man with wise eyes offered them shelter in his humble abode, sharing stories of resilience and hope. His voice cracked with the weight of his own past, his words a soothing balm to their troubled spirits. He had lost loved ones to the very adversaries they now faced, and his determination to stand against them ignited a flicker of hope within Lily and Ethan's hearts.

Their newfound ally warned them of the perils that awaited them ahead, urging caution in every step they took. He spoke of the danger that lay within the secrets they sought to uncover, secrets that powerful forces were willing to kill to protect. His voice trembled as he recounted tales of lives shattered by betrayal, of lives torn apart by the darkness that resided in the hearts of those they trusted.

With a heavy heart, Lily contemplated the true nature of the world they inhabited. She had always believed in the inherent goodness of people, but now doubt seeped into her thoughts like a poison. Could they trust anyone in this treacherous web they found themselves entangled in? Was there anyone left whose loyalty could be relied upon?

Ethan's hand clasped tightly around hers, a silent reminder of their shared resolve. Together, they vowed to push forward, to brave the storm that threatened to consume them. The allies they encountered along the way may be few, but their spirits burned with a fierce determination to expose the truth and restore justice to a world drowning in darkness.

As they resumed their journey, the weight of the secrets and the fear of betrayal bore down upon them. Every step carried them further into the heart of danger, yet they refused to falter. Lily and Ethan were not mere pawns caught in the twisted game of power and deceit; they were beacons of light in a world enveloped by shadows.

Their determination grew with every obstacle they overcame, every sacrifice they made. Their unwavering bond became their greatest strength, shielding them from the relentless storms that raged around them. The more they faced the adversaries who sought to destroy them, the more resolute they became in their pursuit of truth.

Together, Lily and Ethan vowed to unearth the secrets, no matter the cost. They would face the betrayal that lurked at every corner, undeterred by the treacherous web that threatened to ensnare them. For in the midst of darkness, their love and unyielding spirit burned brighter than ever, a beacon of hope to guide them through the most treacherous of trials.

As Lily and Ethan delved deeper into the heart of the treacherous web, the air grew heavy with anticipation. Their footsteps echoed through the forgotten corridors of an ancient labyrinth, each stride a testament to their unwavering resilience. The walls whispered with secrets, the very foundation of their mission, and they vowed to unveil the truth, no matter the personal toll it exacted.

Their encounters with adversaries grew increasingly dangerous, the stakes rising with each confrontation. Dark figures lurked in the shadows, their eyes gleaming with malice. Lily's heart raced as she felt the weight of their gaze upon her, an icy chill tracing its way down her spine. The web of betrayal tightened its grip, threatening to suffocate the flickering flame of hope within her.

In a moment of vulnerability, doubt gnawed at Lily's soul like a ravenous beast. She wondered if their fight was futile, if their struggle against the encroaching darkness was merely an exercise in futility. Tears welled in her eyes, threatening to spill over and extinguish the last embers of her resolve.

It was then that Ethan's voice, filled with unwavering determination, pierced through the veil of her despair. "We may be tested, Lily, but we mustn't surrender. Our journey is not in vain, for the truth we seek is worth every sacrifice." His words, infused with a fierce passion, rekindled the fire within her heart.

Together, they braved each treacherous encounter, their spirits unyielding in the face of adversity. They found allies in unexpected places, individuals who had suffered at the hands of the same dark forces that now threatened their lives. Each ally, scarred by betrayal and loss, bolstered their determination, becoming a living testament to the resilience of the human spirit.

As Lily and Ethan delved deeper into the heart of the web, they unearthed fragments of the truth. Each revelation, like a dagger to their souls, tested their emotional fortitude. They bore witness to the depths of human depravity and the devastating consequences of unchecked power. Yet, even amidst the darkness, glimmers of hope emerged, fragile and delicate as a dew-kissed flower.

They discovered the strength to forgive those who had succumbed to the seductive allure of the treacherous web, understanding that even the strongest among them could be ensnared in its clutches. Their hearts ached with empathy for those who had strayed, recognizing that redemption was within reach if they were willing to face the consequences of their actions.

The journey was not without scars, both seen and unseen. Lily and Ethan carried the weight of their experiences, etched into their souls like ancient glyphs. Yet, they also carried the indomitable spirit of those who refused to be silenced by fear. Their love burned with an intensity that surpassed the trials they endured, a beacon of resilience that illuminated their path.

As they approached the final confrontation, the treacherous web tightened its grip, threatening to entangle them forever. But in their hearts, a fierce determination blazed, unyielding to the darkness that sought to engulf them. Lily and Ethan, bound by their shared purpose and unwavering love, stepped into the heart of the web, ready to face their ultimate test.

For in the face of danger, betrayal, and the unknown, it is in the depths of our emotions that we find our true strength. It is through resilience, forged in the fires of adversity, that we rise above the treacherous web and reclaim our destiny. And so, Lily and Ethan, their hearts intertwined, ventured forward, their souls aflame with the unwavering conviction that love and truth would prevail.

Chapter 6: Ties That Bind

The room fell silent, as the weight of their newfound truth sank in. Lily and Ethan stood there, their eyes locked in a mixture of disbelief and profound sorrow. What had started as a tumultuous affair between two broken souls had now taken a turn they never could have imagined. The betrayal of their spouses had drawn them together, but this revelation went beyond the boundaries of their own shattered marriages.

Tears welled up in Lily's eyes, blurring her vision of the world around her. Her heart, already bruised by infidelity, now shattered into countless pieces. The thought that she had found solace in the arms of her own flesh and blood filled her with an unimaginable sense of despair. How could life be so cruel, so merciless? Each breath felt heavier than the last as

the magnitude of their shared secret sank deeper into her consciousness.

Ethan, too, stood there, stunned and speechless. His whole existence had been turned inside out in a single moment. The revelation that the woman he loved, the woman who had understood him like no one else, was not only his lover but also his long-lost sister tore at the very fabric of his soul. It was a cruel twist of fate, an unyielding blow to his already fragile heart. He felt his knees weaken beneath him, and he clutched at his chest as if trying to physically contain the pain.

The room seemed to close in on them, as if the walls themselves were suffocating them, squeezing out the last remnants of hope and happiness they had managed to find. Lily's thoughts raced back to their shared childhood, the innocent years they had spent apart, completely oblivious to the bond that lay hidden beneath the surface. She felt a pang of guilt, as if her heart had been stained by the forbidden love they had unknowingly embraced.

Ethan's mind, too, was a whirlwind of emotions. Memories of his mother's warm embrace, his father's deep voice, and the home he had known as a child crashed into him like a tsunami of grief. The foundation of his identity crumbled beneath him, leaving him stranded in a sea of uncertainty. The love he had felt for Lily suddenly felt forbidden, tainted by the blood ties they could no longer deny. What were they to do now? How could they navigate this treacherous terrain without losing themselves completely?

Lily reached out a trembling hand, wanting to touch Ethan, to reassure him that they were still in this together. But she hesitated, her fingers hovering in the air, trapped in a moment of paralyzing indecision. The very touch that had once brought them solace now carried an indescribable weight—a reminder of the forbidden love they had shared, of the barriers they could never cross.

Ethan's eyes met Lily's, their gazes locked in a poignant mixture of pain and longing. He understood the depth of her agony, and his heart ached in response. The love they had nurtured, the connection they had believed was unique to them, now seemed like a cruel joke played by destiny. It was a bond that could never be fulfilled, a love that could never be openly acknowledged. In that moment, they both knew that they had to let go, to surrender to the truth that had been unearthed.

As tears streamed down their faces, Lily and Ethan held each other for one last time. Their embrace was filled with sorrow and regret, a bittersweet farewell to the love that had blossomed amidst chaos. They whispered silent promises of eternal support, a commitment to help each other navigate the aftermath of this devastating revelation. With trembling lips, they exchanged a final goodbye, their hearts heavy with the weight of their shared secret.

of their souls, Lily and Ethan carried the burden of their intertwined fates. They knew that moving forward meant relinquishing the romantic love they had discovered in one another. Their connection had become a bittersweet memory, a forbidden chapter in the story of their lives.

Days turned into weeks, and weeks into months, but the pain lingered. Lily and Ethan sought solace in therapy, in the company of friends who understood the complexity of their situation. Together, they embarked on a journey of healing, not only from the shattered relationships with their spouses but also from the shattered dreams of a future they had once envisioned together.

In their shared pain, they discovered a newfound bond, one rooted in compassion, empathy, and an unbreakable sibling love. They became pillars of strength for each other, navigating the treacherous waters of grief and self-discovery. They dove deep into the depths of their own identities, questioning the very essence of who they were and what their place in the world would be.

Lily found solace in the realization that her connection with Ethan was not solely based on romance. She had discovered a brother, a person who understood her deepest wounds, her fears, and her dreams. In Ethan, she found a confidant, a partner in this newfound journey of self-reconciliation. Their bond became a beacon of hope, a reminder that even in the darkest of moments, love could be found in the unlikeliest of places.

Ethan, too, embarked on a profound transformation. The longing he had once felt for Lily took on a different form, one that transcended the boundaries of romantic love. He began to appreciate the strength of their shared bloodline, the resilience that ran through their veins. Their connection became a source of inspiration, a testament to the power of family and the ability to rise above adversity.

As time passed, Lily and Ethan emerged from the shadows of their shattered lives, their hearts scarred but stronger. They learned to redefine their identities, to embrace the complexities of their past while forging a new path forward. Through their pain, they discovered the resilience of the human spirit, the capacity to love and forgive despite the immense challenges they had faced.

Their story became a tale of redemption, of finding light in the darkest of places. Lily and Ethan became advocates for healing, sharing their experiences with others who faced similar tribulations. They championed the power of self- discovery, urging others to embrace the truth of their own stories, no matter how painful they may be.

In the end, Lily and Ethan realized that their shared secret, as devastating as it had been, had served a greater purpose. It had shattered the illusions they had clung to, forcing them to confront their own vulnerabilities and insecurities. It had brought them face to face with the raw, unfiltered truth of their lives, propelling them toward a journey of self- acceptance and self-love.

Their love story may have been tainted, but the bond they had forged as siblings remained unbreakable. Through the depths of their despair, they had discovered an unyielding resilience, a strength that could weather any storm. And as they embraced the complexities of their intertwined past, they found solace in the knowledge that their shared bloodline would forever connect them, guiding them toward a future where love, in all its forms, would prevail.

Chapter 7: Torn Hearts and Shattered Dreams

Lily stood alone in the dimly lit room, clutching a bundle of letters to her chest. The weight of her emotions bore down on her, threatening to engulf her in a sea of despair. The truth had come crashing down, unraveling the fabric of her once idyllic life. Tears welled up in her eyes, blurring the words on the pages, a painful reminder of the betrayal that had shattered her heart.

Ethan, her beloved Ethan, had confessed to an affair that had been kept hidden in the shadows for far too long. Their lives, their dreams, everything they had built together, now hung precariously in the balance. The promises they had made, the vows they had taken, seemed like distant echoes in the face of this devastating revelation.

She felt a tumultuous mixture of anger, sadness, and confusion welling up inside her. How could this have happened? What had gone wrong? Lily's mind raced with questions, the answers to which she feared might only lead her further into the depths of despair.

As the weight of the truth settled upon her, a glimmer of understanding flickered within her wounded heart. The affair was not merely about those letters they had exchanged, but rather about the resilience of their hearts. It was about the love they had shared, the love that had been tainted and tested, yet somehow survived amidst the wreckage of their shattered dreams.

With trembling hands, Lily wiped away her tears and took a deep breath. She knew that she had a choice to make – a choice that would shape not only her own future but also the fate of their relationship. It was a daunting decision, one that required immense courage and vulnerability.

Slowly, she walked towards the door, the weight of her emotions pulling at her with every step. The hallway outside felt suffocating, the air thick with unspoken words and unresolved emotions. Ethan stood there, his face etched with regret and pain, his eyes searching hers for forgiveness.

Their gazes locked, and in that moment, time seemed to stand still. Lily saw the love that had once burned so brightly between them, flickering weakly but still present. She saw the vulnerability in Ethan's eyes, the desperation for redemption. Her heart ached, torn between the pain of betrayal and the glimmer of hope that still lingered.

In the midst of her anguish, Lily realized that forgiveness was not a weakness but a testament to the strength of her love. She understood that love was not perfect, that it was flawed and prone to mistakes. But it was also resilient, capable of mending even the deepest of wounds if nurtured with care and compassion.

Tears streamed down her face as she extended a trembling hand towards Ethan. It was a gesture of forgiveness, an offering of a second chance. Words were unnecessary at this moment; their eyes spoke volumes, carrying the weight of their shared history and the promise of a future rebuilt upon the foundation of their love.

Ethan's shoulders sagged with relief as he stepped forward, embracing Lily with a desperate tenderness. Their tears mingled, their hearts entwined in a dance of sorrow and healing. In that embrace, they found solace and the courage to face the arduous journey of rebuilding what had been broken.

As they held each other, Lily and Ethan knew that their path would not be easy. They had chosen the road less traveled, one filled with uncertainty and doubt. But they also knew that true love was worth fighting for, worth the pain and the sacrifices.

With their hearts now laid bare, Lily and Ethan embarked on the treacherous path of love, forgiveness, and self- discovery. The road ahead would test them in ways they never imagined.

The days turned into weeks, and weeks into months, as Lily and Ethan embarked on their arduous journey of healing. Their once vibrant home became a sanctuary of introspection, where each moment was a chance to rebuild trust and redefine their love.

They sought guidance from therapists and counselors, their words often punctuated by tears and raw vulnerability. Through their shared pain, they discovered the power of communication—the kind that peeled away layers of resentment and fear, laying bare the truth and the deep-seated emotions that had led them astray.

In the midst of their healing, Lily grappled with the delicate balance between forgiveness and self-preservation. The wounds were still fresh, leaving scars that pulsed with pain at unexpected moments. But she realized that forgiveness was not a single act; it was a continuous choice, a commitment to let go of the past and open herself up to the possibility of a future together.

Ethan, too, confronted the consequences of his actions. His guilt weighed heavy on his shoulders, a constant reminder of the pain he had inflicted on the woman he loved. He poured his heart into self-reflection, determined to understand the root of his betrayal and the steps needed to rebuild the shattered trust.

Together, they peeled back the layers of their relationship, examining its cracks and weaknesses. They discovered the importance of empathy and compassion, of truly seeing and understanding each other's needs. It was through this process of introspection that they realized their affair had not been born out of a lack of love, but rather a lack of communication and emotional intimacy.

As their hearts gradually mended, they made a pact to nurture their love with newfound dedication. They created rituals of tenderness, small gestures that spoke volumes of their commitment—a handwritten note left on a pillow, a gentle touch during a vulnerable conversation, or a stolen glance filled with unspoken apologies.

Yet, despite their progress, doubt and insecurity lingered in the corners of their minds. Fear whispered in their ears, tempting them to question whether their love was strong enough to endure the scars of betrayal. In those moments, they clung to the fragments of hope they had painstakingly pieced together, reminding themselves that their love was not defined by the pain they had experienced, but by the strength and resilience with which they chose to face it.

Slowly, the wounds began to heal, leaving behind scars that told a story of resilience and growth. Lily and Ethan recognized that their love, though forever changed, had the power to evolve into something stronger and more resilient than before. They discovered that forgiveness was not an eraser, but a balm that soothed the ache and allowed them to move forward, hand in hand.

In time, their love became a testament to the human capacity for growth and transformation. They no longer defined themselves by the mistakes of the past but by the lessons they had learned and the paths they had chosen. Their journey of self-discovery became intertwined, as they encouraged and supported each other in becoming the best versions of themselves.

With their hearts now scarred but open, Lily and Ethan emerged from the depths of their pain, forever changed and forever grateful for the chance to rewrite their story. They understood that their love was a precious gift—one that had been tested, reshaped, and ultimately strengthened by the storm they had weathered together.

As they stood at the threshold of a new beginning, they knew that the road ahead would still hold challenges. Yet, armed with their love, forgiveness, and a newfound understanding of the depth of their connection, they faced the future with hope and the unwavering belief that their love story was far from over.

Days turned into nights, and nights into weeks, as Lily and Ethan traversed the labyrinthine path of rebuilding their lives. Along their journey, they encountered moments of profound vulnerability and breathtaking strength.

In the quiet hours of the night, Lily found solace in the pages of her journal. Her pen danced across the paper, pouring out her innermost thoughts and fears, releasing them into the realm of the written word. Writing became her refuge, a sacred space where she could explore the depths of her emotions and give voice to the anguish that threatened to consume her.

Ethan, too, sought solace in his own way. He embarked on a pilgrimage of self-discovery, immersing himself in the realms of literature and philosophy. Each word he devoured provided a fragment of wisdom, guiding him towards understanding and redemption. Through the works of great minds, he unearthed the universality of human frailty and the infinite capacity for growth.

Together, they embraced the pain, daring to confront the darkest corners of their souls. It was in those moments of shared vulnerability that they discovered the transformative power of empathy. They learned to hold space for each other's pain, offering gentle reassurances and unwavering support. No longer were they adversaries, but allies in a battle against the ghosts of their past.

In the crucible of their love, forgiveness became a radical act of defiance against despair. It was a process fraught with uncertainty and moments of doubt, but they persisted. They had come to realize that forgiveness was not a singular act but a continuous commitment to choose love over resentment, compassion over bitterness.

In their quest for redemption, they unearthed the forgotten fragments of joy that had once illuminated their lives. They sought solace in shared laughter and rediscovered the simple pleasure of holding hands. These small moments became the foundation upon which their love was rebuilt, brick by brick, until it stood stronger and more resilient than ever before.

Yet, as they navigated the winding path of healing, they encountered obstacles that tested the very core of their commitment. Waves of doubt crashed against the shores of their hearts, threatening to erode the progress they had made. Old wounds reopened, and the weight of their history threatened to pull them under.

It was during those tempestuous moments that they discovered the true measure of their love. They faced the tumult head-on, refusing to allow the scars of their past to define their future. Together, they weathered the storms, clinging to each other with a fierce determination.

Through the haze of tears and the depths of their pain, they began to see the beauty in the imperfections. Their love story was no longer one of fairy tales and unattainable perfection but a tapestry woven from the threads of resilience, forgiveness, and growth. They found strength in their brokenness and, in turn, healed the fractures that had threatened to tear them apart.

As the seasons changed, a new chapter began to unfold—a chapter marked by the triumph of love over adversity. Lily and Ethan stood before their loved ones, their hands clasped tightly together, their eyes brimming with tears of gratitude and hope. They exchanged vows that carried the weight of their journey, promising to honor the lessons learned and to nurture their love for the rest of their days.

Their scars bore witness to the battles they had fought, the demons they had conquered. The room filled with the collective sighs of their loved ones, who had witnessed the transformation firsthand. Each person present knew that this union was not born out of naivety but of a hard-won love that had been tested and emerged stronger.

With their lives now intertwined once more, Lily and Ethan embarked on a new adventure—one that embraced the inherent fragility of the human heart and the beauty that could arise from its mending. They approached each day with a renewed sense of gratitude, cherishing the love that had emerged from the ashes of their pain.

Together, they sought to redefine their relationship, weaving a tapestry of trust, understanding, and unconditional acceptance. They recognized that rebuilding was not a linear path; there were still moments of doubt and insecurity that threatened to undermine their progress. But they faced those moments head-on, their unwavering commitment bolstered by the lessons they had learned and the love that had been fortified through the trials they had overcome.

As they ventured into the unknown, Lily and Ethan discovered that their journey was not solely about rebuilding their own bond but also about extending compassion and forgiveness to themselves. They had both made mistakes, and acknowledging their own fallibility allowed them to release the weight of guilt and embrace the transformative power of self-love.

Their hearts, though scarred, grew bolder and more open. They became beacons of resilience, shining light onto others who were navigating their own tumultuous paths. Together, they sought to spread a message of hope and healing, reminding others that even in the darkest moments, love had the power to transcend pain and rebuild what had been shattered.

In time, Lily and Ethan found the courage to revisit the letters that had first unveiled the truth. No longer symbols of betrayal, those pages became testaments to their growth, reminders of the strength they had cultivated through their shared journey. They read them aloud, embracing the emotions that surfaced, allowing the words to ignite discussions that further deepened their understanding of one another.

The process of rebuilding their lives extended beyond their relationship. Lily and Ethan nurtured their individual passions and pursued personal growth, recognizing that self-discovery was an integral part of their shared path. Lily poured her heart into her art, finding solace and catharsis in the strokes of her paintbrush. Ethan, too, delved into his own passions, embracing his innate curiosity and allowing it to guide him toward new horizons.

With time, the wounds of the past began to fade, replaced by a newfound appreciation for the beauty of imperfection. Their love, though tested, bloomed in the face of adversity, reminding them that vulnerability was the wellspring from which true connection could flow. They allowed themselves to be seen, baring their souls to one another without fear of judgment or rejection.

And so, their story continued, written in the ink of resilience and redemption. Lily and Ethan understood that their journey would forever be a work in progress, a testament to the fluidity of love and the ever-changing nature of the human spirit. They walked hand in hand, their footsteps echoing with the lessons of their past, as they embraced the uncertainty of the future.

Their lives had been forever altered, their hearts forever marked by the scars of their shared history. But within those scars, they found strength, compassion, and an unwavering commitment to the power of love. Together, they forged a path of authenticity and grace, inspiring others to embrace the complexities of their own stories and find solace in the transformative power of forgiveness.

And as they navigated life's joys and sorrows, Lily and Ethan understood that their love was not defined by the absence of pain, but rather by the depth of their resilience and their unwavering commitment to grow, evolve, and cherish the beautiful tapestry they had woven from the threads of their shattered dreams.

Chapter 8: In the Depths of Heartbreak

Lily clutched her heart, her body trembling with a mixture of pain and uncertainty. The truth had ripped through her, tearing apart the fabric of her once idyllic life. The echoes of Ethan's confession reverberated in her mind, drowning out all other thoughts. She stood at the precipice of a newfound understanding, a revelation that threatened to consume her entirely.

In the aftermath of betrayal, Lily found herself in a tempestuous sea of emotions. Anger and hurt collided within her, their waves crashing against her fragile spirit. She had believed in their love, cherished the bond they had forged through countless shared moments. Now, it seemed like a mirage, a figment of her imagination that had shattered with a cruel reality.

Ethan, too, stood on the precipice of his own emotional abyss. Regret gnawed at his soul, a relentless ache that mirrored the pain etched across Lily's tear-stained face. He had kept secrets, hidden truths that had festered beneath the surface, poisoning the foundation of their once unbreakable love. Now, all he yearned for was redemption, a chance to mend the shattered pieces of their connection.

Days turned into nights as Lily and Ethan navigated the treacherous landscape of their wounded hearts. Their conversations were raw and filled with anguish, the weight of their shared journey heavy upon their shoulders. In the silence of their brokenness, they found solace in each other's presence, a flicker of hope amidst the devastation.

Lily's tears became the embodiment of her pain, each drop falling like a testament to the depth of her sorrow. But with each tear shed, a catharsis began to take root within her wounded heart. Through the haze of anguish, she began to glimpse the possibility of forgiveness, a balm for the wounds inflicted upon her trust. The complexities of the human heart had become painfully clear, its capacity for both immense love and agonizing despair laid bare before her.

Ethan, too, embarked on a journey of self-discovery. He had to confront the demons that had led him astray, the choices that had threatened to destroy the very essence of their love. Nights turned into moments of reflection as he delved into the recesses of his own soul, searching for answers and seeking redemption. The depths of his remorse were immeasurable, but within that darkness, he found a glimmer of hope—a glimmer that whispered of a love worth fighting for.

As they walked the path of healing, Lily and Ethan wove the threads of vulnerability into the tapestry of their renewed connection. The scars of betrayal would forever mark their story, a testament to the trials they had overcome. But love, the enduring force that bound them together, refused to be extinguished. It shone brightly, illuminating the path toward forgiveness and redemption.

In the quiet moments, as the sun dipped below the horizon, casting hues of gold and crimson across the sky, Lily and Ethan found solace. Their hearts, once shattered and fragmented, began to heal. They discovered the power of resilience, the strength that can emerge from the depths of heartbreak. In the space between their breaths, they forged a bond that was not only stronger than before but also tempered by the fire of their shared journey.

Ultimately, Lily and Ethan emerged from the darkness stronger, their hearts etched with the scars of their past. They had weathered the storm, fought against the odds, and learned that even amidst the tumult of betrayal and secrets, love and redemption could prevail. Their lives were forever changed, their hearts forever marked by the complexities of the human experience. But as they held each other's hands, they knew that together,they could face any challenge that lay ahead.

It was not an easy road they traveled. Trust had been shattered, and rebuilding it brick by brick required unwavering commitment and an unwavering belief in the power of love. Lily and Ethan had to confront their deepest fears, laying bare their vulnerabilities and insecurities. But they were determined to rise above the wreckage of their past and create a future where honesty and understanding prevailed.

Days turned into weeks, and weeks turned into months as Lily and Ethan embarked on a journey of self-discovery and mutual growth. They sought therapy, both individually and as a couple, to navigate the labyrinth of their emotions. Through tear-stained sessions and heartfelt conversations, they learned to communicate with openness and compassion, unraveling the layers of hurt that had entangled their hearts.

The path to redemption demanded sacrifices. It demanded that they face their own shortcomings and make amends. Ethan, in particular, dedicated himself to making things right. He embraced his role as the architect of change, determined to prove his unwavering commitment to Lily. He showered her with gestures of love and kindness, knowing that rebuilding trust required patience and consistency.

Lily, too, grappled with her own demons. Forgiveness was not a linear process, and there were moments when the wounds of betrayal threatened to resurface. But she drew strength from the love they shared and the growth she witnessed in Ethan. In those vulnerable moments, she reminded herself that true strength lay in embracing the scars of the past and forging ahead with hope.

As time passed, the jagged edges of their pain began to soften, slowly but surely. Love became their refuge, a sanctuary where wounds could heal, and hearts could mend. The complexities of the human heart, once a source of anguish, became a wellspring of understanding and empathy. Lily and Ethan recognized that their journey was not just about salvaging their relationship, but about embracing the imperfections that make us human.

And so, they emerged from the depths of heartbreak with a newfound appreciation for the fragility and resilience of love. Their lives had been forever altered, and scars would remain as a testament to their past struggles. But those scars, instead of defining them, became symbols of their triumph over adversity.

Lily and Ethan's story became a beacon of hope for those who had stumbled upon the rocky terrain of betrayal. Their love, though battered, stood tall as a testament to the enduring power of forgiveness and redemption. They had learned that even amidst the darkest moments, there lies a flicker of light—a flicker that, when nurtured and cherished, can illuminate the path to healing and create a love that is stronger than ever before.

As they gazed into each other's eyes, Lily and Ethan knew that their journey was far from over. But armed with the truth, a newfound understanding of the complexities of the human heart, and a love that had weathered the storm, they faced the future with unwavering determination. Together, they embraced the challenges that lay ahead, knowing that their love had been tested and had emerged unbreakable.

Lily and Ethan stood at the precipice of a new beginning, their hearts intertwined by the trials they had overcome. They had weathered the storm, emerged from the depths of despair, and now, they stood united, ready to embrace the future with open arms.

The scars of their past had not faded entirely, but they no longer held the power to define their love. Instead, those scars served as a reminder of their resilience, a testament to their unwavering commitment to growth and understanding. Each

scar told a story of redemption, a story of a love reborn from the ashes of betrayal.

Together, they embarked on a journey of rebuilding, weaving new threads into the fabric of their relationship. They nurtured a culture of transparency and open communication, knowing that trust could only flourish in an environment of honesty. Their shared experiences had taught them the value of vulnerability, and they embraced it, baring their souls to one another without reservation.

Lily and Ethan discovered the beauty of rediscovery. They dove headfirst into exploring the depths of their individual selves, encouraging one another to chase their dreams and aspirations. Their shared journey became a catalyst for personal growth, as they recognized that their love thrived when they nurtured their own passions and supported each other's ambitions.

It was in the simple moments that their love truly flourished. A gentle touch, a lingering glance, or a heartfelt embrace held more significance than grand gestures. They found solace in the mundane, cherishing the everyday experiences that reaffirmed their deep connection. It was in those moments of quiet intimacy that they realized the true strength of their love, forged through the fires of adversity.

As time passed, the wounds of the past gradually faded into the background, replaced by a profound appreciation for the present. Lily and Ethan no longer dwelled on the pain of betrayal, but instead focused on the lessons it had taught them. They understood that love, like a fragile flower, required constant nurturing and care. They were committed to tending to their relationship, watering the seeds of trust and affection with unwavering dedication.

Their renewed love radiated warmth, touching the lives of those around them. Friends and family marveled at the transformation, witnessing the power of forgiveness and the resilience of the human heart. Lily and Ethan became beacons of hope, proof that love could conquer the darkest shadows and rise anew, stronger than ever before.

Together, they faced the challenges that inevitably crossed their path. Life was never without its obstacles, but they approached each trial hand in hand, drawing strength from their shared history. No longer were secrets and betrayal lurking in the shadows; instead, their love shone brightly, a beacon guiding them through the storms of life.

Ultimately, Lily and Ethan knew that their journey was not about reaching a destination but rather about embracing the beauty of the ever-evolving path. They had come to understand that love was not a stagnant entity, but a living, breathing force that required continuous nourishment and growth. And they were committed to embracing that journey, with all its uncertainties and triumphs.

As they stood on the mountaintop, gazing into the horizon, Lily and Ethan were filled with a profound sense of gratitude. They had traveled through the depths of heartbreak and emerged on the other side, reborn and renewed. Their lives were forever changed, their love forever transformed.

With a renewed understanding of the complexities of the human heart, Lily and Ethan embarked on a future filled with endless possibilities. They no longer feared the trials that lay ahead, for they knew that their love and redemption would prevail. They had learned that even amidst the darkest moments, love could rise, phoenix-like, from the ashes, resilient and beautiful.

Hand in hand, they stepped forward, ready to face the world as a united front. Their love, once fragile and tested, had now become a source of strength and inspiration. They knew that the road ahead might not always be smooth, that challenges and temptations would inevitably arise. But armed with the lessons they had learned, they approached those obstacles with unwavering commitment and a newfound wisdom.

Lily and Ethan sought to make a difference in the lives of others, driven by the transformative power of their own experiences. They became advocates for open communication and forgiveness, sharing their story with those who yearned for hope in the face of adversity. Through speaking engagements, support groups, and online platforms, they reached out to those who had lost faith in love, offering a guiding light to help them navigate their own turbulent journeys.

In the process of healing, Lily and Ethan discovered the true essence of empathy. They had walked the path of betrayal and knew the pain it inflicted, but they also understood the potential for growth and redemption that lay within. They extended their hearts to others, offering compassion and understanding to those who had experienced similar heartaches. Their love story became a beacon of hope, inspiring others to believe in the power of second chances.

The complexity of the human heart no longer frightened them; instead, it intrigued them. They celebrated the layers of emotion and understood that love, at its core, was a beautifully messy tapestry woven with joy, pain, and everything in between. They embraced the imperfections of their own hearts and embraced each other with a profound acceptance that came from truly knowing one another.

In their shared journey, Lily and Ethan forged a bond that transcended the boundaries of time and circumstance. Their love became a refuge, a sanctuary where they could find solace and strength, a safe haven from the storms of life. They had learned that true love was not about perfection, but about resilience, forgiveness, and unwavering commitment to growth.

Years passed, and as Lily and Ethan looked back on their shared journey, they marveled at the distance they had traveled. Their love had defied all odds and emerged victorious. They had faced the depths of heartbreak and emerged with a love that burned brighter than ever before.

And so, they continued to walk hand in hand, their steps guided by the lessons of their past. Their story remained a testament to the power of love and redemption, a beacon of hope for those who faced their own tribulations. Lily and Ethan understood that their journey was not merely their own; it was a story of resilience and triumph that resonated with the hearts of many.

As they faced the world together, their love shone as a reminder that even amidst the complexities and hardships of life, love and redemption could prevail. They were living proof that from the depths of heartbreak, a love reborn could become a force that defied all odds, forever changing the lives of those who embraced it with unwavering faith.

And so, they walked on, hand in hand, ready to face whatever lay ahead. With hearts filled with love and gratitude, they embraced the beauty of the present, confident that their love would continue to evolve, grow, and inspire others on their own journey of healing and renewal. Their story would forever be etched in the annals of love, a testament to the enduring power of the human heart.

Chapter 9: Unveiling the Betrayal

Lily's hands trembled as she held the faded photograph in her grasp. It was a relic from the past, a fragment of a shattered truth that threatened to consume her. The revelation she and Ethan had unearthed pierced her heart like a thousand daggers. Their investigation had taken an unexpected turn, leading them down a path of darkness that reached far deeper than they could have ever imagined.

Gathering her strength, Lily turned her gaze towards Ethan, who stood by her side. His eyes mirrored her turmoil, mirroring the anguish etched upon his face. Together, they faced a truth that demanded sacrifice and reckoning, a truth that tore at the very fabric of their souls.

"It can't be true," Lily whispered, her voice barely audible. "Our parents...they were part of this sinister organization. How could they betray us like this?"

Ethan's voice wavered as he replied, his voice laden with grief and confusion. "I don't know, Lily. But we have to face the truth, no matter how painful it may be."

The weight of their parents' betrayal bore down upon them, threatening to crush their spirits. The once-familiar memories of laughter and love now mingled with the bitter taste of deception. Lily felt a wave of anger surging within her, tinged with a sense of helplessness. How could they have been so blind to the evil lurking beneath their own roofs?

As they dug deeper into their parents' involvement, the pieces began to fall into place. The clandestine organization had preyed upon their families, weaving a web of deceit that ensnared their parents in its sinister machinations. Lily's heart ached with each revelation, as if her very core were being ripped apart.

"I can't believe this," Lily choked out, tears streaming down her face. "Our parents...they ruined our lives, all for their own selfish desires."

Ethan's hand found its way to Lily's trembling shoulder, offering solace in their shared pain. His touch provided a glimmer of warmth amidst the coldness of their shattered trust. Together, they would navigate the storm of emotions, seeking justice for the lives that had been torn asunder.

"Our parents' actions do not define us, Lily," Ethan said, his voice filled with determination. "We will rise above this darkness and find a way to make things right. We owe it to ourselves and to those who suffered because of their choices." Lily wiped away her tears, her resolve ignited by Ethan's words. She knew they had a daunting task ahead, a battle against an organization that had infiltrated their lives with meticulous precision. But she would not let despair consume her. She would channel her pain into a fire that burned brighter with each passing moment, fueling their pursuit of justice.

As they prepared to face the organization head-on, a newfound strength blossomed within Lily and Ethan. Their journey had transformed from a mere investigation into a personal quest for redemption. They would confront the sins of their parents and ensure that the shadows cast upon their lives would never darken another soul.

Together, they stepped into the unknown, their hearts aflame with a burning desire for truth and justice. The path ahead would be treacherous, but they were no longer alone. Lily and Ethan had found solace in one another, forging a bond stronger than the secrets that threatened to tear them apart. And with unwavering determination, they marched forward, ready to confront the sinister organization and uncover the full extent of their parents' betrayal.

Lily and Ethan stood at the precipice of their mission, their hearts heavy with the weight of their parents' betrayal. The road ahead was fraught with danger, uncertainty, and a sea of unanswered questions. But they had each other, and that would be their guiding light through the darkest of nights.

With a resolute determination etched on their faces, they began to unravel the intricate web spun by the clandestine organization. Their pursuit of truth took them to the depths of forbidden secrets, unearthing a hidden world of corruption and malevolence that lay just beneath the surface.

As they dug deeper, Lily's emotions intensified. The anguish of her shattered trust mingled with an overwhelming sense of grief for the parents she once cherished. The tendrils of betrayal coiled tightly around her soul, threatening to suffocate her with bitterness and despair.

Ethan, too, battled with conflicting emotions. Anger surged through his veins like a raging inferno, threatening to consume him. The revelation of his parents' involvement had shattered his perception of family, leaving him adrift in a sea of doubt and anguish. Yet amidst the tempest of emotions, he found solace in Lily's unwavering presence.

Together, they found strength in their shared pain. They leaned on one another, their bond growing stronger with every step they took towards the heart of darkness. In their eyes burned a flicker of hope, a belief that even amidst the ruins of their lives, redemption was within reach.

Days turned into weeks, and weeks turned into months as Lily and Ethan delved deeper into the organization's secrets. They uncovered a sinister plot that extended far beyond their parents' involvement—an intricate web of power, manipulation, and unbridled greed that ensnared the innocent.

Each revelation tore at their souls, but they refused to waver. Their pursuit of justice had transformed into a mission to protect others from the clutches of the organization. Their pain had become a catalyst for change, fueling their unwavering resolve to dismantle the nefarious web that had ensnared their families.

The battle to expose the truth was not without its sacrifices. They encountered danger at every turn, facing adversaries who would stop at nothing to protect their secrets. But Lily and Ethan remained undeterred, fueled by an unyielding determination to bring their parents' actions to light and restore some semblance of justice to their shattered lives.

As they confronted the leaders of the organization, Lily and Ethan found themselves standing on a precipice once more —a precipice of redemption. The truth lay before them, waiting to be unleashed upon a world shrouded in darkness.

With every word spoken, every piece of evidence presented, the weight of their parents' actions grew lighter. The organization's power waned in the face of unwavering determination and an unyielding belief in justice.

In the end, the truth prevailed. The secrets that had tormented Lily and Ethan were exposed, and their parents' sins laid bare for all to see. It was a bittersweet victory, for the wounds inflicted upon their hearts would forever leave scars. But through their pain and resilience, they had triumphed over the darkness that threatened to consume them.

As they stood amidst the ruins of their shattered lives, Lily and Ethan held onto each other, their hands entwined. They had emerged from the crucible of betrayal stronger and wiser, with a renewed appreciation for the fragility of trust and the power of resilience.

Their journey had come full circle, and though they could never erase the pain of the past, they had found a measure of closure. Together, they would forge a new path—one built on the foundation of their own resilience and the unbreakable bond they shared.

Their journey had come full circle, and though they could never erase the pain of the past, they had found a measure of closure. Together, they would forge a new path—one built on the foundation of their own resilience and the unbreakable bond they shared.

As the dust settled, a profound emptiness lingered within Lily and Ethan. The truth had set them free, but it had also stripped away the illusions they had clung to for so long. They grieved not only for the loss of their parents' love but also for the innocence they had once possessed. The weight of the world seemed to rest upon their weary shoulders.

In the midst of their pain, they found solace in each other's arms. The tenderness of their embrace whispered promises of healing and hope, gently mending the shattered pieces of their souls. They realized that their journey had never been solely about vengeance or exposing the truth—it was about reclaiming their own identities, rebuilding their lives on a foundation of honesty and resilience.

Together, Lily and Ethan embarked on a path of healing and self-discovery. They sought therapy to untangle the emotional knots that had entwined their hearts, allowing themselves to grieve the loss of the parents they once thought they knew. It was a process filled with tears, anger, and moments of profound vulnerability, but they faced it head-on, determined to find their own peace amidst the ruins.

During their healing journey, they encountered others who had fallen victim to the organization's machinations. Lily and Ethan realized they were not alone in their pain. United by shared trauma, they formed a support group—a sanctuary where broken souls could mend together, finding strength in their shared experiences.

Through their newfound connections, Lily and Ethan discovered a profound purpose in their own healing. They became advocates for justice, shedding light on the hidden stories of others and empowering them to reclaim their voices. In their vulnerability, they found strength, and in their scars, they found resilience.

The road to redemption was not without setbacks. The scars of betrayal occasionally resurfaced, triggering moments of doubt and despair. But Lily and Ethan knew that healing was not a linear process. It was a journey of peaks and valleys, of forward strides and occasional stumbling. And with unwavering support for one another, they pressed on, refusing to let their past define their future.

Years passed, and the pain gradually transformed into a deep sense of empathy and understanding. Lily and Ethan had forged their own path, driven by a shared mission to bring light to the darkest corners of human existence. They channeled their pain into acts of compassion, creating organizations and initiatives that provided support and resources to those affected by betrayal and manipulation.

Their parents' actions had set their lives ablaze, but from the ashes, Lily and Ethan had risen, stronger and more resilient than ever before. The scars that adorned their hearts were reminders of their triumph over adversity, symbols of the indomitable spirit that had carried them through the storm.

As they stood on the precipice of a new dawn, Lily and Ethan looked back on their journey with a mixture of gratitude and sorrow. They had paid a heavy price for the truth, but it had set them free—free to rebuild their lives, free to rewrite their stories, and free to embrace a future defined by love, authenticity, and the unbreakable bond they shared.

And with hopeful hearts, they stepped forward, knowing that no matter what challenges lay ahead, they would face them together, forever bound by the redemptive power of their love.

Chapter 10: Super Time Travelers Unleashed

Lily's heart pounded against her chest as she stood in the dimly lit room, her hand tightly clutching Ethan's. The weight of their mission bore down on them, each step they took amplifying their shared determination. They were not just siblings; they were warriors united by a burning desire for justice. Their eyes locked, and in that moment, they understood the gravity of what lay ahead.

The room buzzed with an undercurrent of whispered conversations and sly glances. This was the heart of the organization they sought to dismantle—a place where evil thrived behind a facade of respectability. Lily and Ethan, draped in the shadows, had infiltrated this den of malevolence, masquerading as pawns in a wicked game. They played

their parts to perfection, their masks hiding the fire that raged within.

With every passing day, Lily's heartache grew deeper. She had witnessed firsthand the organization's cruelty—innocent lives ripped apart, dreams shattered, and hope extinguished. Her emotions welled up inside her, an amalgamation of anger, sadness, and an unwavering thirst for retribution. But it was Ethan who kept her grounded, his steady presence reminding her why they were here.

Ethan's grip on her hand tightened, his eyes reflecting an unspoken understanding. No words were needed; their bond transcended mere blood ties. They shared a past filled with memories of laughter, tears, and unbreakable loyalty. Now, their connection was fortified by a shared purpose—a mission that demanded everything they had to offer.

As they moved through the labyrinthine corridors of the organization's headquarters, each step brought them closer to the truth. The faces around them were masks of deceit, their smiles disguising the darkness within. Lily and Ethan exchanged glances, silently acknowledging the dangers that surrounded them. They were two lone souls navigating treacherous waters, but together they were a force to be reckoned with.

Their journey led them deeper into the organization's inner circles, their true identities cloaked by a web of lies. They were the pawns now, willingly dancing with the devil, all in the name of justice. Every interaction, every whispered conversation, was a tightrope walk, teetering between discovery and success. But they knew the risks, and they embraced them willingly.

Lily's heart trembled as they stumbled upon a hidden chamber—a repository of the organization's most damning secrets. The room held a collection of horrors that made her stomach churn. The weight of it all threatened to crush her spirit, but she refused to back down. These secrets were the keys to dismantling the organization, to exposing the malevolence that thrived in the shadows.

Their hands trembling, Lily and Ethan began to document the evidence—the proof that would change the world. As they sifted through the documents and photographs, tears welled in Lily's eyes. She was overwhelmed by the enormity of the task before them, the weight of justice resting solely on their shoulders. The lives they had lost, the lives yet to be saved —it all hinged on their success.

In that room, the siblings became more than just warriors; they became the voice of the voiceless, the hope of the hopeless. Their hearts beat as one, pulsating with an indomitable will to right the wrongs that had plagued their lives. Their bond, forged in the crucible of adversity, burned brighter than ever.

As they left the hidden chamber, Lily and Ethan carried with them the truth—the ammunition to bring down the organization. They knew the risks that awaited them—the enemies who lurked in the shadows, ready to strike at their weakest moments. But they were prepared to face them all, for they had found strength in each other. The fire that fueled their souls burned fiercely, igniting an unyielding determination to see their mission through to its end.

As they ventured deeper into the heart of darkness, Lily and Ethan encountered obstacles they never could have imagined. Betrayal lurked around every corner, and danger whispered in their ears like a seductive serpent. But their bond, woven from the threads of trust and love, shielded them from despair.

In the darkest of nights, when the weight of their burden threatened to crush their spirits, Lily found solace in Ethan's eyes. His unwavering belief in their cause was an anchor that kept her grounded. With every beat of their hearts, they reinforced their resolve, vowing to protect the innocent, even at the cost of their own lives.

Their days blurred into nights, and nights melted into days as they toiled relentlessly, gathering the final pieces of evidence. Their hearts ached for the victims whose stories had gone untold, but they knew that soon, justice would prevail, and their voices would be heard.

The time came to unveil the truth—a truth that would shake the foundations of the organization, leaving no stone unturned. Lily and Ethan prepared for their grand reveal, their nerves intertwining with a sense of liberation. They had fought tooth and nail, sacrificed their own safety, and navigated a treacherous labyrinth. Now, they would unleash the storm they had meticulously brewed.

As the world held its breath, waiting for the unveiling of secrets, Lily and Ethan stood side by side. Their eyes met one last time, acknowledging the magnitude of their accomplishment. They had transformed themselves from mere siblings into warriors of righteousness, their hearts etched with the scars of battles fought and won.

The room fell into a hushed silence as Lily's voice, charged with emotion, pierced the air. Every word carried the weight of the innocent lives that had been shattered, the dreams that had been stolen. With each revelation, the world watched in horror, the truth crashing upon their souls like a tidal wave.

Tears streamed down Lily's face as she bared her soul, exposing the organization's darkest secrets. The room trembled with the collective gasp of realization, and a symphony of emotions swirled through the air. The truth had been unleashed, its power shaking the very foundations of the organization.

In that moment, Lily and Ethan knew they had fulfilled their purpose. They had chipped away at the fortress of darkness, allowing the light of truth to seep in. The journey had been arduous, but their spirits remained unbroken. Their bond, born in the crucible of their shared mission, had grown into an unbreakable force.

The world would forever remember their names as symbols of bravery and resilience. Lily and Ethan, two souls bound by blood and a relentless pursuit of justice, had changed the course of history. With their hearts still heavy from the pain they had witnessed, they took solace in the knowledge that their sacrifice had not been in vain.

As they embraced each other, tears mingled with smiles, for they knew their mission was complete. Driven by a desire for justice, they had dismantled the organization from within, unearthing the truth and exposing the darkness that lurked in the shadows. And in doing so, they had not only found justice for the victims but also redemption for their own wounded hearts.

Epilogue: Echoes of Triumph

The world erupted in a chorus of outrage and disbelief as the revelations spread like wildfire. The organization that had thrived in secrecy and manipulation was now exposed for all to see. Lily and Ethan's bravery had pierced through the veil of deceit, leaving an indelible mark on the annals of justice.

In the aftermath, a wave of change swept across nations, as the truth ignited a spark of collective resistance. People, inspired by the resilience and determination of two siblings, rose up to demand accountability. The echoes of Lily and Ethan's triumph reverberated through society, awakening a new era of transparency and righteousness.

Yet, amidst the accolades and the transformation, Lily and Ethan found solace in the quieter moments—the ones that reminded them of the lives they had touched and the lives they had saved. The victims, once silenced, now found their voices. They reached out to the siblings, sharing their stories of healing and newfound hope. These encounters became a balm for Lily and Ethan's souls, reaffirming their purpose and reminding them of the profound impact they had made.

Their own scars remained, etched deep within their hearts, but they carried them as badges of honor. The weight of their mission had forged them into warriors, tempered by the fire of adversity. And as they moved forward, hand in hand, they knew their journey was far from over.

Lily and Ethan became advocates, dedicating their lives to empowering those who had been silenced. They traveled far and wide, speaking out against injustice, and lending their strength to those still trapped in the clutches of darkness. Their story became a beacon of hope, a testament to the power of unity and resilience.

Their bond, once forged in the shadows, grew stronger with each passing day. They had emerged from the crucible of their mission not just as siblings, but as kindred spirits, bound by an unbreakable love and an unyielding commitment to justice. Through the highs and lows, they found solace in each other's unwavering support, a constant reminder of the strength that resided within them.

As time wove its tapestry, the world changed, and so did Lily and Ethan. The shadows of their past became a distant memory, replaced by the bright light of a future filled with purpose and possibility. They continued to fight for justice, armed with the lessons learned from their harrowing journey.

And in the depths of their souls, they knew that their story was not just their own. It was a story of resilience, of the human spirit's capacity to overcome even the darkest of trials. Lily and Ethan's legacy would endure, forever etched in the hearts of those whose lives they had touched.

The world would forever remember the siblings who dared to challenge the powerful, who risked everything for the sake of justice. Their bond would forever serve as a reminder that, in the face of adversity, love and determination can conquer even the most insurmountable of odds.

And so, as Lily and Ethan stepped into the unknown, hand in hand, they embarked on a new chapter—a chapter filled with the promise of a better world, where justice would prevail and the echoes of their triumph would reverberate for generations to come.

Don't miss out!

Visit the website below and you can sign up to receive emails whenever Richard Porter publishes a new book. There's no charge and no obligation.

https://books2read.com/r/B-A-TGVE-EUEJC

BOOKS 2 READ

Connecting independent readers to independent writers.

Did you love *Whispers of Deception Bloodlines Unveiled*? Then you should read *Shadows of Redemption: A Tale of Love and Transformation*[1] by Richard Porter!

"Shadows of Redemption: A Tale of Love and Transformation" is a captivating novel that explores the unlikely alliance between Nathan, a notorious drug lord, and Emily, a brilliant chemist. When Nathan recognizes the potential of Emily's groundbreaking new drug, he sees an opportunity to legitimize his criminal empire and build a new life for himself. As they work together to refine the drug and navigate the treacherous world of organized crime, they find themselves drawn to each other in unexpected ways. But the path to redemption is riddled with danger, and they must confront their dangerous associates and the shadows of their past to forge a new future together. This gripping story

---

1. https://books2read.com/u/4AA7nN

2. https://books2read.com/u/4AA7nN

delves into themes of love, resilience, and the power of second chances, as Nathan and Emily strive to escape their dark past and create a brighter tomorrow.

About the Author

I have been writing short stores for 5 years.

Now I find people, love, them, Keep your eye out for more from Porter.